WOODY AND JUNE
VERSUS THE WANNABE
WARLORD

WOODY AND JUNE VERSUS THE WANNABE WARLORD

WOODY AND JUNE VERSUS THE APOCALYPSE, EPISODE 1

ROBERT J. MCCARTER

LITTLE HUMMINGBIRD PUBLISHING

WOODY AND JUNE

VERSUS

THE APOCALYPSE

Woody and June versus the Wannabe Warlord

Woody and June versus the Apocalypse, Episode 1

Copyright © 2019 by Robert J. McCarter

Cover photography © 2018, Robert J. McCarter

"Zombies Ahead" image by ducu59us

Version 1.0, February 2019

ISBN: 978-1-941153-05-5

Find out more about this book at: WoodyAndJune.com

Visit Robert's website at: www.RobertJMcCarter.com

Published by:

Little Hummingbird Publishing

P.O. Box 23518

Flagstaff, AZ 86002

www.LittleHummingbird.com

Little Hummingbird Publishing is a division of Arapas, Inc. Find more about Arapas at: www.Arapas.com.

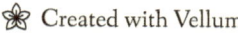 Created with Vellum

CHAPTER ONE

MAYBE YOU'RE SMARTER than I am. Maybe you get up in the morning with a clear direction for your day. Knowing what you want to do, having a clear list of things to get done, and checking them off one at a time. Like this:

1) Kill a few zombies for exercise; the apocalypse doesn't mean you can stop doing cardio.

2) Outwit a psychotic, petty, wannabe warlord freeing your little group from his or her (the apocalypse is equal opportunity) cruel grasp.

3) Find enough food, water, and medicine to get through the day.

4) Lead your hearty band to shelter where you can sleep and not worry about zombies or psychotic, petty, wannabe warlords.

Yeah, you probably are smarter than I am.

I guess my day has a list of sorts, but with only two things on it:

1) Survive, and...

2) Laugh, 'cause what is surviving without at least a slice of joy. Oh yeah, and one addendum to item two: Don't laugh like a psychotic, petty, wannabe warlord because then you would just suck.

Mwahahas are strictly off limits. Also cackling, and schadenfreude is frowned upon. We're looking for real laughter here.

I say all of this as preface to my tale so maybe you'll get where I'm coming from. And, you know what? I do know that you are smarter than me, because you actually have the time and leisure to sit down and read my story. Well, I hope someone reads this, I really do. So, if you are reading this, that makes you way smarter than me—or existing in the post-post-apocalyptic world where zombies have been eradicated, and well, that makes your ancestors smarter than me.

A character in a story, me in this case, my name is Woody, has to have a problem. My problem is staying alive. Every day that's my problem. It can get a bit monotonous. At the opening of this story it seems just like another day full of checking off my short list of survival and laughter. I awake to a cold morning, my shoulder and hip aching, the sun just peeking up over Interstate 40 above a ridge of pine trees.

"Shit," I say, because that is the proper way to greet a post-apocalyptic morning. Especially when you wake up on top of a semitrailer, your body sore like you've just been through a dryer cycle, your mouth drier than the Sahara, and your stomach as desolate as... enough damn metaphors, you get the idea. All of that is true, but the "shit" is mostly because I can hear the Zs weakly banging on the trailer I took refuge on. They know my fresh brains and delicious entrails are up here just waiting for them to eat.

Ironically, they, the zombies, have the same problem I do. Survival. Although they never laugh—ever—which is one of the reasons why it's second on my list (of two things, so don't be thinking yourself all cool, number two). You see, a zombie needs to eat, too, or they will dry up like a mummy and eventually blow away. Problem is, it takes about four years (a wild guess at this point) for a Z to starve to death, and it takes me about thirty days. That makes trying to wait them out fairly unworkable. Besides, the Zs continue to feast on the living, making the end date of their reign of terror further and further out.

I push myself up into a sitting position, yawn, roll my shoulders trying to loosen them up, put my baseball cap on, and look around. I'm in the loading area of a dog food factory on the east side of Flagstaff, Arizona, camped out on the top of one of twenty semi-trailers parked there.

I'm a Phoenician, but let me tell you that the dry, hot, flat desert is no place to be during a zombie apocalypse. This is experience talking. Not unless the idea of living in a world dominated by the undead is just too much for you and you'd just as soon get it over with. Then, well, the Valley of the Sun is just a fine place, but I digress. Again.

Back to the cold morning in May on top of that semitrailer, the Zs milling below me. I get myself standing and stretch my aching body some more, pulling my army surplus jacket tight—who says you can't look like a badass after the world ends?

Once I loosen up a bit, I check two things, and I can be rather obsessive about this. The first is my Arizona Diamondbacks baseball cap. It's red with the logo of a rattlesnake curled into a "D" in black. This is kind of my touchstone to my past and my humanity. I love baseball, I was an all-star in high school, played in the minors briefly, but tore my rotator cuff and never got back to it. And now... well, if humanity survives, it will be a while before baseball gets much attention.

The other thing is the packs of seeds zipped in the inside pocket of my jacket. This is food and the future, hope really. I've got carrots and beans and lettuce. It's not much, not enough, more of a symbol. You gotta have something to keep you going out here.

I move slowly, wanting to stay quiet so I don't attract more of them, and get a count of how many I'm up against.

"Shit," I whisper, because some things just need utterance, even when you don't have anyone to talk to. There are twenty of the beasts, all hungry for my deliciousness. It seems I attracted all the Zs in the area last night when I took refuge up here. Noisily and ungracefully, I might add. Do you have any idea how hard it is to get on the top of one of these things? It's not like there's a ladder or anything. I lucked out and there was a big pickup that ran into it, so that kinda saved my life—because it was getting dark and the Zs spotted me as soon as I got here.

I'm on the south side of the building, the walls are made of cement in a corrugated pattern about thirty feet tall. Two towers rise up above it and behind those, Mount Elden, which is my destination. I'm up on an isolated trailer in the parking lot, nothing close by except for that pickup.

I finally made it up to Flagstaff yesterday evening. I-17 joins I-40 up here and the bulk of the town sits around that. When the infection hit, I tried the whole survival-as-a-group in the city where there is lots of food to scrounge for, but it got ugly. When number one on my list, survival, looked doubtful, I found a truck and as much food and water as I could and headed out.

I didn't have that truck very long and that is a story for another day, but suffice it to say that in this new world, if you have something worth taking, someone will take it. Now, I have a general policy of not having anything worth taking and to have nothing to do with anyone else. Groups just get messy and fast.

If I'm telling the truth, and I'm trying my best to do that, Phoenix got more than ugly, it got weird... I got weird... but I'm not ready to write about that yet.

I spent a lot of time in the North Country as a kid, my dad was born here and we visited a lot, so I know my way around. After the disaster of getting out of Phoenix, I left the highway and got here on foot, with nothing worth taking. There are Zs out there in the forest, but not that many. There are some people too, so I kept moving, slowly but surely, to the north. Out of the desert. Farther away from any population centers. Which brings us to Mount Elden. It's steep and rugged, rising over two thousand feet up above Flagstaff. On top is the Mount Elden Lookout Tower with a set of stairs no Z could ever manage.

Yeah, I know. It's something worth having so someone is going to want to take it, but I have some fond memories of my old man and me hiking up to it when there was an actual ranger there and he let us in to take a look at the magnificent view. The San Francisco peaks to the northwest, the painted desert east and south, the ponderosa pine forest all around.

Maybe I won't stay. Maybe I'll climb up and shed a tear for our lost world and my dead father. Maybe no one will have thought of going there and I'll get to stay for a while. There are lots of isolated areas up here, I'll find one to wait it out. And, actually, the lookout tower is not the best candidate because there is no water up there— and this being Arizona, not much water anywhere.

But I gotta try.

"Hey, dummy!" a voice calls.

My heart skips a beat and suddenly I'm awake. I'm confused, but I'm sure it's not my own voice. I mean, I've been alone for way too long, not talking at all, but I do still recognize the sound of my own voice.

And this is definitely a female voice and it's not often that my own sounds that way.

CHAPTER TWO

I LOOK AROUND, trying to find the voice that is not mine, which I should have been doing instead of such introspective navel gazing. The call came from the roof of the dog food plant. It's a girl, short black hair, dirty face, blue jacket. Not much else I can tell from this distance.

"Good morning," I yell back. "I must tell you that I plan to be lodging a complaint with management. The room service around here really sucks."

Well, that just wakes the Zs up and they start moaning and groaning, a few of them trying to climb up the truck that crashed into the trailer, but quickly failing and falling back down. Zs are dumb and slow, which is the only reason there are any living left.

"You're funny," she says, with no humor whatsoever in her voice. I revise my estimate up from girl to young woman and remind myself of my strict go-it-alone policy.

"Thank you very much," I say, taking off my hat and bowing. "I'll be here all week."

"Yeah, you will. Want some help?"

I look down, and I am surrounded by zombies, especially around the truck, which is the only safe way down. There are a few more of them shambling their way towards me, our conversation having alerted them to the possibility of breakfast.

"No thank you," I yell back.

"Suit yourself, then. I'll grab some popcorn and watch the show." She pauses briefly and even from this far away I can see that she is smiling. "And by 'popcorn,' I mean dog food. There's actually some left if you manage to survive."

Oh crap, now I officially like her and my stomach growls. Yeah, I know, gross. But it was the reason I made a stop here, the possibility of well-preserved calories that others might not think of. Any calories in an apocalypse, as the saying goes.

"I'll do my best to make it a good show, then."

But I don't, not right away. Showing off for the first female that's spoken a kind word to you in months is a sure way to fail at survival. I eat, which amounts to about a hundred calories of stale crackers and roasted peanuts. I drink the four ounces of water I have left and give it a few minutes. The one concession I make to being watched by a woman is not peeing on the Zs. Oh, and I do use a little bit of that remaining water to brush my teeth. I tell myself that oral hygiene is even more important now with no dentists (and it is), but who am I kidding?

I then dig in my pack, pull out some rope and a pink two-pound hand weight and tie it to the end of the rope. This is going to take a while, but it will be safe.

It goes like this. Find an area with fewer Zs, swing the rope with the weight on it right above their heads. When the alignment is good, let out a couple of inches of rope and bash them in the head. Boom. Down they go. Except it takes a lot of attempts and sometimes a couple of hits per Z. It is slow and tiring, but it's safe.

"You're not dumb," she yells after the first one goes down. "That's kinda refreshing."

"How's the popcorn?" I yell back.

"Delicious!"

I smile and chuckle. Not a belly laugh or anything, but I'll take it.

It takes two hours, but I clear the Zs. She claps. I bow with my hat in hand and then put the hat right back on, containing my over-long, sandy brown hair. I need a haircut, for sure. My beard has gotten rather long in the last few months too.

I put everything away, put my pack on, make sure I've got my knife on my belt—long and thin, perfect for shoving through the eye socket of a hungry Z—, grab my bat, and climb down.

I'm tired and thirsty and dehydrated. To which I say, welcome to the apocalypse. Nothing new.

"Which way in?" I call up. "I'm dying for some popcorn."

She walks above the last loading bay and points down. I eye it. There's still a trailer in it and it will be kind of tight squeezing in. I don't like tight places. It's easy to get trapped in tight places.

I shrug. Nothing to be done about it. "My name's Woody, by the way."

"June," she calls back. After a pause, she adds, "Let me guess, the folks just loved *Toy Story*?"

"Yes, they did!"

I've got a smile on my face anticipating a full stomach—even if it's dog food—as I walk toward the loading dock. I'm keeping an eye on June, because... well... I should. Trust is hard these days, but I watch her mostly because of biology. It doesn't stop for the apocalypse. I've been lonely and as I get closer it becomes clear that she's fairly cute and in her twenties like me. And she's got a sense of humor. This makes her a post-apocalyptic babe.

As I get closer, I hear some banging from inside one of the trail-ers. I stop and stare.

"They're trapped in there," she says. "No worries."

But I *am* worried. What else don't I know about June, about this situation?

"Ummm..." I begin. "I don't mean to be rude or anything, but is there, like, a normal way in? You know, a door, preferably with some glass?"

She shrugs. "Yeah. West side of the building, just go around that way. No idea if any Zs are left over there, but knock yourself out." She starts walking along the roof towards the west.

I stay in the open away from the service road, which parallels I-40, and away from the building. I swing around where I spent the night, plugging my nose against the rotting-flesh-zombie smell of the breakfast crowd I just took out.

As I get past the parking area, the building juts out and the way narrows. I slow down and listen. The wind has picked up and I don't hear anything. I jog along until things open up again and come to a treed area, mostly pines and a few fir and deciduous trees. From her perch above me, June is pointing towards a lower building and I head over.

Being on foot these days is nerve wracking. I prefer heights, the kinds the Zs can't get to. See why that lookout tower is so appealing?

Once in the trees, I slow down and make my way towards the front door, a sidewalk leading up to it.

This is looking to be a good day, but like is often true for the post-apocalyptic world, things can go to crap in an instant. The wind is whipping which is why I don't hear the zombies until they are almost on me. A group of five shambling my way. And they look hungry—but then again, Zs always look hungry—and I'm the only food around.

CHAPTER THREE

I DON'T NEED to do extensive descriptions of these beasts, do I? They move slow with a lurching gait, maybe 1.5 mph at their fastest, like when they think it's dinnertime. They are dirty, stink like rotting meat with a fungal overtone, have glassy eyes, and most have some kind of wound. Guts dangling out, a compound bone fracture sticking out their sleeve, or ribs jutting out their side, that kind of thing. And they hiss and snarl, and moan. Their teeth snap together in anticipation of eating you. Classic zombie stuff. And while I have an ample supply of theories, at this point I don't know much about the science of real zombies, but I'll give you a hint: It's not quite like the TV shows and comics, but just close enough to be freaky.

Well, I see the five and turn around only to see a group of eight heading through the narrow area I just passed through.

Shit.

They must have heard us when I was too busy flirting—hmmm, do I even know what that is anymore? Maybe I was just talking to a member of the opposite sex and at the same time noticing that they were indeed a member of the opposite sex. So, I was too busy maybe-flirting to follow proper survival protocol.

I look to I-40, but there is a fence with three strands of barbed wire on the top, and my way through it was about a quarter of a mile to the east.

I'm trapped.

I tighten my grip on the baseball bat and start thinking about odds. The five are definitely the better bet. I put my odds at 50/50 on getting through.

And then there's a whistle and June yells, "Hey dummy, over here."

I've been on my own for months—on purpose—with no one to rely on, and there wasn't one thought in my brain that this young woman I mighta flirted with would try to help me.

She's at the corner of the building and has thrown a rope over the edge with strategically placed knots—probably how she gets to the roof in a guaranteed zombie-free way.

Both sets of Zs are closing in and shuffling faster. They think they've got me. From the larger group, there's two close to the rope, so I rush to the one that is closest, whack his head with the bat, which makes a gross wet sound like I just bashed a watermelon. As I wind up for the second, he's on me.

You've smelled morning breath, probably some really bad morning breath, I know you have. The breath of a zombie is a hundred times worse than that. Seriously. I've almost died from their halitosis and I'm about to again. The Z grabs me and his exhale makes my eyes water and I have to force myself not to wretch. I'm holding him off with one hand while going for my knife with the other. Zs aren't superhuman strong or anything, but they're not weak either.

He's snarling and his jaw is snapping and two more are almost on me by the time I get my knife and plant it in his left eye. He goes down in a heap. I back up a step, almost to the rope, but two she-Zs are on me then. I go for the bigger one with the knife, but realize too late that the other one is closer. In a most cliched, B-movie way, things slow down. Her mouth opens and moves towards my extended elbow. Here it is, the bite, the infection, the eventual death when...

The second one's head explodes, covering my face with the grossest, stinkiest, most disgusting goo of an undead rotting former human. I don't look, I'm not that dumb, not with more Zs almost on me, but I know June shot her.

I finish off the larger one and scramble up the rope.

CHAPTER FOUR

I FLOP on the roof of the building, my breath coming in ragged gasps from the forty-foot climb—yeah, I might have said the building was thirty feet tall earlier, but I upped my estimate after climbing. These things are relative, you know. Well... at least one's subjective experience of them is, and in this case, mine, and it felt like at least forty feet.

I pull a rag from my pocket and begin wiping the splatter off my face. This is godawful stuff I've got on me. It's stinky, slimy, and tepid. Since zombies run cool, it's noticeably cooler than human norm and that just freaks me out. I rub it off and spit and gag and am anything but graceful, ignoring June for the moment.

It's the zombie goo, you see. I suspect that ingesting too much can be detrimental to my health—especially their brains. Either the bacteria in it will make me too sick to take care of myself and I'll die of dehydration and become a zombie, or it will supercharge the Z-infection we all have, and I'll die and become a zombie.

Life these days is all about avoiding that "die and become a zombie" part.

I actually got lucky. My eyes blinked shut at the right moment and I got very little in my mouth. But I spit and gag and carry on just to be sure.

Don't get me wrong, I am grateful to be alive, but now I'm going to be tasting zombie for the rest of the day. And the taste... If I were trying to make it sound a lot better than it is, I'd say it tastes like moldy, rotting meat. Suffice it to say it tastes a lot worse than that.

"Thanks," I say when I'm done with my ungraceful cleaning. I turn to June and freeze.

She's got a hunting rifle slung over her shoulder—what she must have offed the Z with—and a handgun, a 9mm I think, pointed at me. She's ten feet back and I have no chance if she wants to shoot me.

In the adrenalized moment, I don't stop to consider that if she wanted me dead she could have just left me to the Zs... or shot me instead of the Z. I'm thinking I'm out of the frying pan and into the fire. I'm thinking that I should have fled in the opposite direction as soon as I saw her. Solo survival is hard, the Zs are relentless, but they're not devious like the humans.

"Happy to help," she says with a small smile. "Now divest yourself of all your weapons."

A thin part of my mind, one I just want to kick in the teeth, realizes that she's not just cute, she's CUTE! Round face, olive skin, delicate nose, compelling ocean-blue eyes. She's petite, dressed in jeans and an oversized grey sweater. I'm not sure of her age, anywhere from twenty to thirty. My heart, my stupid heart, starts beating faster.

My bat got abandoned down below, so I slowly pull my knife out of its holster and drop it on the roof. I take my pack off and step away, my hands up. I don't say anything. I don't know enough about what's going on to try to talk my way out of it.

"No guns?" she asks.

I shake my head. Guns are useful, for sure, but they're the kind of thing other people with guns want to take from you, so I don't use them. Oh, and I really hate guns, a past trauma, pre-apocalypse.

"Nothing strapped to your ankles?"

I pull my pant legs up, there's nothing.

She lets out a sigh, the gun lowering a bit, her shoulders slumping.

"Thank you for saving my life, June," I say and really mean it now that I'm not dealing with zombie goo all over my face and in my mouth.

"Sure, Woody."

We stand there in awkward silence and the one thought that keeps roaming through my head is, "God, she's cute." And I do mean "cute" because there is something about her beauty and petiteness that portrays innocence. She's on her own and alive well into the zombie apocalypse, so she's got to be more tough and smart than cute. And believe me, I know this, but I've starved myself of companionship for so long that she's like an oasis in the desert.

"Look..." I begin after the awkwardness has had babies, raised them, and sent them to college. "Trust was never easy, and now..." I shake my head. "There really is no way I can convince you to trust me. Words just don't count. You saved my life, so I kinda trust you."

She nods, her face passive. Our kinda-sorta flirting is out the window now that we are in the same space. That only worked when we were thirty yards away from each other.

"So, you make the rules here. I can go, right now, all I ask is we find me a clear way down."

She nods again, no data there, just a signal to continue.

"Or, if you are being super generous, maybe you can share some of your 'popcorn' with me and let me spend the night up here. I can't imagine there are any Zs on the roof."

She shakes her head, the gun still pointed at me, although it has lowered some more.

"I wouldn't mind, you know, a conversation with someone besides myself," I add.

She cracks a smile.

"Don't get me wrong, I'm a wonderful conversationalist, it's just that I always know what I'm going to say."

She smiles wider, but then it disappears transforming her face into a grim mask. "Woody, if you... I swear, I'll..." The gun is pointed right at my chest now.

"I get it. I swear I do. Tell you what, I won't move unless you tell me to move."

She nods, her face relaxes again.

I hold up my hand, like a first grader trying to get the teacher's attention.

"What?" she asks, clearly a bit exacerbated, her forehead crinkling up, which is totally... cute.

"I gotta take a leak. Can I go pee on some Zs?"

She laughs, a real laugh, and nods towards the edge of the building.

CHAPTER FIVE

DOG FOOD IS... well, it's a bit dry and very bland. On the plus side, it clears the taste of zombie goo but leaves you with dog food breath.

We're in the middle of the large roof. This section has regular skylights, farther to the north and east the roof is covered in solar cells —now that's valuable, but also bait for the psychotic, petty, wannabe warlords in the vicinity. To the north of us there is a small tower and a higher section of the building. At the northwest corner is the tall tower, rising about one hundred feet in the air. It's the tallest building on this side of town and kind of a landmark.

June has some kind of shelter either up here or in the building, but she hasn't shown it to me. She's sitting about ten feet away, her legs crossed and the pistol in her lap. She gave me a mostly empty bag of dog kibble—senior formula, because it's easiest on your guts—and a bottle of water. Both she pulled out of her pack. And I gotta admire that. She's probably been up here for a while but carries her pack at all times just in case. And in the post-apocalyptic zombie world, just in case happens all the time.

"You been here long?" I ask, trying to make conversation around the dry crunching.

She purses her lips. Okay, then, that topic is out of bounds.

I nod to the tower. "Everybody around here knows about this place."

Her eyes narrow, she's thinking carefully about everything I say.

"I'm not going to be your only visitor," I say, making myself clear. "Not having anything anyone wants has served me pretty well lately."

"What kind of life is that?" she asks.

I take a sip of water and swallow. June said to eat this stuff slowly and I am understanding now, it's hard to get down. "It's a life, at least. The Zs have lowered the bar on 'quality of life' quite a bit."

She nods. "So where are you going?"

I point past the tower to Mount Elden rising behind it. "There's a lookout tower up there. I mean, yeah, lots of people know about it, but mostly locals. Someone might be there, but if not, that's a place I could really sleep."

"That sounds like something valuable," she says.

I nod. "Yeah, if a bunch of gun-toters want it, I'll leave. But it's remote, survival up there is not going to be easy. But it is close to this side of town and could be a good sanctuary."

Her forehead crinkles again, cutely I might add, and then she says, "Why are you telling me all this?"

And that is a good question. I shouldn't have, it was violating so many of my rules. I shrug.

"Really," she says, her hand moving closer to her gun. "I need you to tell me."

I sigh. "You saved my life and... I've been kinda starved for human companionship." I feel my cheeks begin to flush as I ponder a different kind of human companionship with the decidedly cute June and wonder what is under those baggy clothes. I dig in the kibble bag as cover.

When I look back up, her blue eyes meet mine. "I get that."

"Wanna go?" I ask before I can even think about it, and I'm sure my cheeks are bright red by now.

She looks away and is still for a moment before getting up, her gun in hand. "Stay there," she says with a smile. "I'll be right back." She jogs off across the roof.

OPTION NUMBER ONE: Run to the rope, grab my stuff, and escape. Continue on this loner path.

Option number two: See what this intriguing pixie woman is going to come back with and violate my guiding survival principals.

I pick option two, slowly munching on dog food and sipping water for ten minutes. It's the best meal I've had in two weeks.

When she gets back, she rips open a cheap candy bar, the kind I would have turned my nose up at pre-apocalypse, splits it in two, and tosses me half. She then steps back and sits down, only six feet away.

"What's this for?" I ask.

"To celebrate. We're going on an adventure."

I'm both surprised and delighted, and scared to death. What have I gotten myself into? We chat then, not about anything pre-apocalyptic and personal, and not about anything too serious. About the weather and TV shows we used to like. Scrounging tips and the weirdest places we've slept (me, I climbed and tied myself onto many a pine tree to rest on the way here; she found dumpsters to work in a pinch). It's fun, like actually fun. A simple, easy conversation. I don't even think about how cute she is... well, not that much anyway.

When the sun starts getting low, she asks me to wait again and comes back with a camping pad and some blankets. I thank her, make a joke about how the hospitality has improved, but she's serious now.

"You stay here, understand?" she asks.

I nod. A big, flat, zombie-free roof with some padding and plenty of blankets sounds about like heaven.

"'Cause if you follow me, if I see you anywhere but here, I'll shoot you. Got it?"

I agree and she walks off. When she's gone, I realize that I have to go to the bathroom, and we didn't cover that, and I really don't want to get shot.

I wait a few hours and sneak to the corner of the building under the cover of darkness and take care of my biological necessities. I then go back to my pad and blankets and sleep like a baby knowing there are no zombies up here.

CHAPTER SIX

FROM THE PET FOOD FACTORY, the trail up Mount Elden is north about half a mile. To get there we have to get down off the building, go past the mall and a bunch of other shops, and cross State Route 89.

As we're eating breakfast—you guessed it, dog food, senior formula to keep you regular—we plan this out. She's six feet away, the gun in her lap, but she's relaxed. We are going to use the rope to get down off the north end of the building and stay in open areas until we get to the trail.

And then it occurs to me. Yesterday when I asked about a way into the building she offered me one of the loading docks. There must be Zs in the building. Was she trying to get rid of me then, but somehow took pity on me when I was about to be bitten?

"What's wrong?" she asks, my face must be showing what I'm thinking. "If the Zs are on the north end, we might have to make a bunch of noise to draw them away, but it will work."

I nod and lick my lips, all the good "she saved my life" vibrations draining out of me.

"What!?" she asks, staring at me.

Trust between two humans has always been a trick. But now... it's a major feat. It doesn't take much to mess it up. I nod back to where she was when we met and tell her what just ran through my mind.

She swallows hard and nods.

"I get that you weren't going to give away any secrets at that point," I say, "but..."

"Most of the Zs are gone, just a few roamers left in the building," she says. "I would have warned you. I swear. You not going for it showed you had your head on and I needed to know that too."

There are thin, high clouds today and the weather is cooler. I draw my army surplus jacket tight. "I get it," I say. "I even respect it. It's just..."

She stares at me, those blue eyes probing, like she's trying to see into my weird brain, and it wouldn't help if she could, believe me. She then nods, picks up her gun, and stuffs it into her pack. She points to my pile of stuff about twenty yards away at the end of the building. "Feel free," she says.

It's an act of trust. I smile, it's a real smile, and thank her.

𝚔𝚊𝚊 𝚢𝚏 𝚊𝚊𝚊

THE FIRST MILE UP towards Elden Lookout Trail is easy, relatively speaking. It's on a trail called Fat Man's Loop, which runs along the side of a deep, rocky gash in the mountain around and between huge boulders. There are short Gambel oaks, a bush that kind of looks like manzanita but with silver bark, ancient alligator junipers, and pine trees, of course.

Flagstaff and the surrounding area, if you've ever been there, is all about the ponderosa pine tree. The forest has other trees, but it is dominated by the pines, large sections of it with nothing else but a few, rare oaks. Tall, with dark brown bark, the ponderosas tend to be fairly symmetrical and are covered in bunches of dark green needles that are quite sharp. The bark is separated into sections by black crevices with the bark on the bigger trees lighter than on the smaller ones and the sections bigger and the crevices deeper. The big trees, if you put your nose near one of those crevices, smell sweet like vanilla.

These trees love the altitude, dry climate, and volcanic soil of Northern Arizona—they absolutely dominate it. It's something you might take for granted, unless you are a desert rat like me and feel yourself relax whenever you are out among them and smell their sweet scent.

Even though I've been living in the forest for many weeks as I made my slow progress north, I'm still delighted when we get out among the trees. Forests feel like safety to me.

The trail name, Fat Man's Loop, seems a bit ironic, given that it's quite steep, until you get past it. After that you are on a series of switchbacks that zigzag up one of the eastern arms of the mountain, and then it gets truly hard. All told, you climb over two thousand feet in less than three miles. Strenuous comes to mind.

It takes us a few hours to get to the trail, nothing untoward occurring, and as we start up the trail we slow down. We hardly talk, we need our ears to listen for Zs or people, and we have to go slow when the forest gets dense.

Down low, we see a few Zs in the forest, but they are at a distance and we don't need to deal with them. Some stretches of the switchbacks have great views and we pause about halfway up and take a break.

Trust has been restored, but it is still tenuous. I go in front, we both seem to want it that way, and she always has her gun in hand.

"How much farther?" she asks, her voice barely above a whisper. A raven flies silently over us, its black wings glistening in the sunlight as it rides the currents off the mountain.

I shrug. "It's been years. Always hard to tell where the top is when you're on the mountain."

"And your plan when we get there?"

"Approach slowly. See if it's occupied. Turn around if it is."

She nods and we lapse into a companionable silence looking out over the east end of Flagstaff and the monster ponderosa pine forest beyond.

🚶‍♂️🚶‍♀️

BACK IN THE LATE SEVENTIES, Elden had a pretty big forest fire. As we get almost to the top and start along a ridge, the tower just visible, that damage is evident. The steep slopes are covered with downed and rotting trees, only small pines taking their place even decades later. I pause, it's an appropriately post-apocalyptic landscape.

I point to the two metal structures visible just above the peak, the lookout station and a microwave communication tower.

She smiles and nods.

I signal for her to follow and take us off the trail and behind a boulder. "Let's rest here and see if we can hear anything," I whisper.

She nods and gets out the "popcorn" and we eat a bit and rest. We haven't seen or heard anything since the few Zs we saw out in the forest at the bottom. I'm feeling good about this plan. I lean back on the boulder and close my eyes so I can concentrate on listening, and because I'm tired. I can feel her next to me, hear her breath and her crunching on the dog food, smell her scent. Which is, to be honest, not the most pleasant scent. Sweat, dust, dog food, and... something else. Something a bit sweet and entirely human. It's distracting.

"I don't hear anything, do you?" I ask after I open my eyes.

She shakes her head. I nod to the trail and we get back to it, our pace slow and careful.

The trail ends on a small, flat-ish area at the peak of the mountain. Right in front of us is the communication tower, thick with microwave antennas which look like huge, oddly shaped drums. On the other side of the open area is a rectangular brick building painted a dark red, and right behind it, the lookout tower rises sixty feet and has a small room on the top and long switchbacking steps going up to it. To our left an old truck is parked.

The clouds have thickened and there's a healthy breeze up here evaporating the sweat from the climb.

No people. No Zs. Sanctuary. A place to feel safe.

I open my mouth to say something, but June grabs my arm and squeezes hard. A man pops up from behind the truck and points a rifle at us. Another one appears from behind the communication tower. I look back down the trail and see a third man.

Shit!

CHAPTER SEVEN

THEY'VE STRIPPED us of our weapons and our packs and walked us down the dirt road a half of a mile or so to a broader, flat area of the mountain where two dirt roads converge. There's a camp setup here with half a dozen tents and three pickup trucks. They've cut down some of the smaller trees and left trunks of some of the bigger ones. On these trunks, they've built watch platforms.

They're in the process of building a barbed wire fence and a line of sharpened sticks buried in the ground and angled out just beyond the fence for the Zs to run into. There's another half-dozen men down here working. I don't see any women.

This camp is not visible from Flagstaff, I studied the mountain and the tower on my way here quite a few times. I never saw a person. It's not visible from the trail we came up either. They are being very careful and this scares me.

On the way in, they dropped our packs at the edge of the camp but kept our weapons. There are three men with guns trained on us while a fourth paces in front of us, his hands behind his back.

June is next to me, her face hard, but I know she's scared, and I know it's my fault, and I feel terrible about it. This camp is situated here for a good reason. They are well hidden. They must have been keeping watch and laid in wait for us after they saw us coming up the lookout trail.

The pacing man, a psychotic, petty, wannabe warlord, I presume, is short and stocky with his brown-going-to-grey hair buzzed like a marine's. His face is decidedly plain, and his brown eyes are flat. He's got a pistol and a knife on his belt. He seems to be waiting for something.

A boy, maybe thirteen, comes running back from the way we came and says to Mr. Short and Stocky, "No signs of anyone else."

He nods, stops pacing, and looks at us. "So, you are alone."

"Yes," I answer, even though it wasn't really a question.

"And what are you doing up here?"

"Just trying to survive," I say. "Sorry to bug you guys. We're happy to move on."

He smiles at me, the kind of condescending look one might give a clueless child. I want to hit him.

He turns to the three men with the guns. "The girl can stay. Shoot him." He walks away towards the largest tent.

And here it is. The moment I've been trying to avoid since I escaped from Phoenix and the psychotic, petty, wannabe warlord that I ended up with down there. I have something they want. June. Not that she's mine, not at all, but she's with me and they want her. They want her for...

"Wait!" I shout. "I know things. I can be useful to you."

He snorts and continues walking.

June's got a hold of my arm again and is squeezing it hard enough to hurt. I know why they want to keep her and not me, and so does she. This world has never been very kind to women, but the apocalypse set things back a ways. And in a weird way, she just saved my life, again. If I had come up here alone they would have killed me once they made sure I wasn't part of a larger group. I can't abandon her to them.

"Gunpowder!" I shout "I know how to make gunpowder. Dynamite, if I have the right ingredients."

He stops, his shoulders relaxing as he turns around. "Dynamite?"

"You're going to need more firepower."

He raises an eyebrow and nods for me to continue.

"You probably know this, but there's a big group that has cordoned off part of the university... NAU. They've got a complete chem lab, books, and people who know what they're doing. So yeah, dynamite. You're going to need it. It's not easy, it'll take some serious scrounging and some time. But, short term, I have some ideas on where we can find some. But I need—"

He's back in front of us and the look on his face stops me short. I was about to ask for something and he knew it.

"...but I was thinking, maybe you need gunpowder first," I continue, covering up my ask. "Ammo won't last forever, and that's easy."

He shakes his head. "Bring me dynamite. You have twenty-four hours."

Things have changed. He wants something and he is willing to trade for it. So far, he's offered time, but maybe he is willing to offer more.

"I need seventy-two hours and your promise that she remains unharmed."

He smiles at June, it's a leering, lecherous look that makes me want to strangle him. "No harm will come to her," he says.

June spits on him and he just smiles wider. "I like spirit in a woman," he says. He must be twice her age and now I want to beat him senseless.

"No one touches her and we both go free," I say.

"Twenty-four hours," he says, looking at his watch. I glance at mine; it's almost 4:00 p.m.

He nods to one of his men, a big guy, at least two hundred fifty pounds. He comes over and grabs June, and she promptly punches him in the face, bloodying his nose. He pulls back his arm to hit her and I jump on him.

A shot rings out and we all freeze.

Mr. Short and Stocky is angry, his cheeks flushed red. "Twenty-four hours. You have my word, no one will touch the scrawny little girl." He looks like he just ate something sour and now I want to kick him in the balls. "But, she must cooperate."

I look at June, her nostrils flaring and her blue eyes dark with rage, but she nods. I don't say anything, just hold her gaze for a few breaths, hoping she can see how sorry I am that I got her into this and how hard I'm going to work to get her out of it. My much-vaunted, go-it-alone survival rules are in a shamble. It's not about me anymore.

"Agreed," I say. I then turn and run up the dirt road back toward the trail. Twenty-four hours isn't very long. I pass our packs along the way and grab them without asking.

I don't have much time.

CHAPTER EIGHT

HERE'S what I've figured out about Mr. Short and Stocky, our psychotic, petty, wannabe warlord. He's not dumb, look at the way he set up his camp up and lay in wait for us. But he's not that educated, either. Making dynamite, the key ingredient being nitroglycerin, is not something done easily or quickly, and not something I have any clue how to do. The gang at NAU—that part wasn't a lie—can. Me? Nope.

His plan for us is also clear. He is risking nothing right now. If I come back with dynamite he might keep me, leverage my attachment to June to get more. Either way, neither of us is getting away.

My attachment to June... Shit. There it is. Entanglements, those things get you dead in this world. And I've known her just a day and a half.

Maybe I should forget about her and just keep running. Sure, she saved my life, and yeah, she's cute and all, but survival is rule number one. But am I that big of an ass? Has a life of survival changed me that much?

All these things run through my mind as I tear down the trail much faster, and much noisier, than I should. I'm not leaving her. I need to get some supplies and I need to get somewhere safe before dark. I need to make some dynamite, knowing how be damned.

FIGHTING ZS, surviving the close calls, getting through the day with your life is... Well, it's a mess of adrenaline, you might even say it makes you feel "alive," but it ain't living. Racing through a post-apocalyptic town, dodging Zs, breaking into an office supply store, a car dealer, and then a Home Depot in a desperate plan to save another human being... Now that's adrenalized and stressful, and not the kind of thing you want to do every day, but it *is* living.

Despite my tired brain and exhausted body, I realize this on my climb back up to Elden Lookout Tower the next day. Maybe this won't work, maybe we are both going to die—or worse—but the last three days have been the best three days in a long, long time.

As I crest the trail with a backpack in my right hand and my left hand hidden in the sleeve of my jacket, I see them.

Mr. Short and Stocky and six other beefy boys are standing on the dirt road in front of the towers waiting for me. Half of them are wearing dark-green army surplus jackets and I resolve to change my look if I survive this. If army surplus jackets are the fashion trend with the psychotic, petty, wannabe warlord set, I definitely need another look.

June is there. She looks okay. My heart is racing because I know our odds aren't good.

The psychotic, petty, wannabe warlord looks at his watch and nods. "Punctual, I like that."

I just nod and walk until I'm eight feet away. "Let her go and it's all yours," I nod to the pack in my hand.

I'm sweating, partially because of the climb and the sunny day, partially because my jacket is zipped all the way up, and partially because I'm scared to death.

He looks at me. I know he's wondering whether there is really anything in that pack. I see his brain turn as he studies me. I don't have any visible weapons and I didn't even have a gun yesterday. There are seven of them, there is no way for us to get away. He has nothing to lose.

He nods to the linebacker holding June and he lets her go. She walks slowly towards me, and when she's halfway there, I toss the pack most of the way towards them. Attached to the zipper is a small black box with a blinking red light. It was hidden from them before by the way I held the pack.

June trots the next few steps and is right beside me. I can smell her sweat and her fear, and that something a little bit sweet. That June-ness.

"You okay?" I ask, keeping my eyes on Mr. Short and Stocky who walks forward to the pack.

"Yeah. You got a plan?"

I nod and unzip my jacket with my right hand while pulling my left hand out of the sleeve. There's a quick intake of breath by one of the beefy boys when he sees me, and then a few more as they all notice. I've got on a vest with wires, red LEDs, and about thirty sticks of dynamite strapped to it. Glued to the dynamite is an array of small nails and screws. In my left hand is a hacked-up handle off a leaf blower with more red lights and my thumb firmly on a red trigger.

"Nobody make any fast moves," I say. A total cliché, I know, but I'm hoping it'll work with this group of cliched post-apocalyptic survivors.

June swears under her breath when she sees what I've done.

"I'm hoping we all survive the day, but I am happy to take you all with me if it looks like I'm not going to."

June's staring at me, her eyes wide. "Where'd you get the—" I can see it, she's not buying it and afraid she just gave my bluff away.

"Out east on I-40," I answer. "I remembered they had a construction site there, redoing a bridge out by Padre Canyon." I shrug. "Got lucky."

Mr. Short and Stocky looks at me, his bland brown eyes drilling into mine, his face flushing red with anger. "What's in the pack?" he asks.

"Same thing that is strapped to my chest. It's also wired to this dead man's switch and full of screws and nails so it's got a pretty good lethal range. When that light stops blinking," I nod at the device attached to the pack, "it's safe to open. Something happens to me, something happens to her, or you open the pack too soon, and..." I end with a shrug. "We get away, you get your dynamite. A deal's a deal."

He's looking at me again, but there is some curiosity in his eyes now. It appears he his reappraising me. Trying to find a way to keep the dynamite and keep us. His boys, though, are looking very nervous.

I don't give him time to think. I take June's hand and take a step back. She catches my eye, looking young and scared, but there is curiosity there too. She's also wondering if I'm not who she thought I was. I'm not sure if that is a good thing when she gives my hand a small squeeze.

Mr. Short and Stocky and his boys aren't moving. They're staring at us. They're buying this, at least for now. We back up, slowly, until we are out of sight, and then we turn and run. I don't take my hand off the dead man's switch and I don't let go of June.

CHAPTER NINE

WE'RE down the ridge and starting on the switchbacks, our breath coming fast, before June starts asking questions. "What!? How did you do all this? Is that really dynamite—"

"Wait," I say, stopping and letting my breath catch up a bit. I widen my eyes and add, "I've had four of those 5-hour energy drinks in the last day, no sleep, and am kinda shaky." I pointedly look at the dead man's switch. "I'll tell you everything when we are safe. I promise."

She nods and I know I've scared her, probably more than I need to, but I'm pretty sure they have scouts on the trail and walkie-talkies. I have no idea if we're safe yet.

We keep moving, and when we're about halfway down the switchbacks I lead us off the trail and into a canyon. I smile when I see the pack I left on the way up, that's a good sign. I nod towards it. "Water and a gun for you. If you see anyone shoot them."

She nods and we both drink before scrambling down the canyon. When it's less steep, I take us to the southeast until we hit a trail and take that to a residential neighborhood. There a beat-up Ford Focus is waiting.

"You better drive," I say, getting in the passenger's side door. After June gets in, I add, "Get us out of the neighborhood and head north on 89." I then drop the dead man's switch and slouch down into the seat, my breath coming in ragged gasps, my heart pounding in my ears. We are alive. By some miracle, we are alive. A hysterical laugh escapes me and my hands are shaking like two fall leaves in a heavy wind that are barely clinging to their tree. June doesn't say a word but drives.

It's not fast going, there are abandoned cars, but they're not hard to get around. When we get out of town, I have her turn on Townsend Winona Road.

"They can see us," she finally says. "That damn tower. I know they can see us."

"I'm counting on it. I'm expecting Mr. Short and Stocky to track us the whole way."

"Mr. Short and Stocky?" she asks.

I nod. "Yeah, you know, the psychotic, petty, wannabe warlord. Did you get his name?"

She shakes her head and snorts. "No, I just thought of him as Asshole."

I laugh, it's a bit high pitched and just a tad hysterical, but I'll take it as my laugh for the day. "I love it. My name for him was a boring physical description, and yours was a tart commentary on how he presents himself to the world."

She's not laughing, but at least there's a smile. "So, you gonna tell me everything now?"

"Can we survive the day first?" I ask, ripping my coat and then the fake suicide vest off and tossing them both in the back.

She purses her lips, tightens her grip on the steering wheel, and nods.

CHAPTER TEN

WE'RE on I-40 heading east, crossing the bridge over Padre Canyon, the sun just having set. We had to deal with Zs a few times along the way, but nothing too difficult, and I've got to tell you, June is good with a gun. Being on the move as we were, and in such a hurry, we didn't worry about noise. In fact, if we attracted more Zs in our wake, so much the better. We both know they're going to follow. Psychotic, petty, wannabe warlords just can't help themselves.

And while June is cute and that petiteness and round face can portray innocence, that's not who she is. She's tough and competent and clearly has had some training with guns.

Her eyes widen as she sees the construction equipment and trailer on the east side of the highway.

"Did you check?" she asks.

"Yeah. No dynamite, not that I had much time to search. Given how far they can see from up there I had to have a real construction site. Pull in here," I say, pointing at Twin Arrows Trading Post, a sad white building with peeling paint and two gigantic arrows out front sticking into the ground.

The trading post was abandoned long before the apocalypse and is barely standing. Nothing here, no reason for anyone to be here. I have her pull the Focus behind the building out of sight of the mountain. There is a shiny new pickup truck there. It's jet-black with four-wheel drive and a crew cab. The bed is full of supplies and the tank full of gas.

I even found some gas treatment to add to the tank. At some point, before we run out, the gas is all going to go bad. Best enjoy it while it lasts.

June just stares at me, her forehead crinkled in that decidedly cute way. "Now. Spill."

I nod. "Fake dynamite. Got paper from an OfficeMax along with string, and then some wax to make the paper look realistic and glue. Scrounged electronics from tools at Home Depot. Got sand for the 'dynamite,' nails, and everything else there too. Used a lot of glue. Drank way too much caffeine. Drove out here last night without any headlights and a scooter in the back of the truck. Drove the bike back in the dark. Survived numerous encounters with Zs. Climbed the damn mountain for the second time in two days. Bluffed my ass off, and here we are!" I end with a big smile on my face and tip my hat to her.

She looks like she's about to cry. "What's next?"

I nod to the truck. "After it's dark and before the moon comes up, we double back the long way, staying off the road we came in on, which they will be using at some point. We then head north on 89A. They're coming after us, we both know that, but we won't be here. I'm thinking the high desert, past Wupatki National Monument, down by the Little Colorado River. There's no tower, of course, not much in the way of buildings, but there were never many people out there, and there is water."

She nods and sniffs. I wrack my exhausted brain trying to figure out why she's upset, what I missed. A crying woman is for me, like many men, akin to kryptonite; it just makes us weak. It was a decent plan, pulled off in short order, and actually, unbelievably, worked.

There's more danger right around the corner, but that's just life in the post-apocalyptic world.

"Hey, cheer up," I say. "We outwitted a psychotic, petty, wannabe warlord today. We're alive. We're not..." And then I pause and start to understand why she's near tears. "...and we're not alone. We've got..."

My words hang in the air as her blue eyes look deep into mine. Tears well up in her eyes, but don't quite spill, unlike me. The tears are flowing, and I don't know that I care. Today was the first day I really lived in a long time, and I'm still alive.

She sniffs, nods, takes a deep breath, leans over and... kisses me on the cheek. "Thank you, Woody," she says.

I nod. "Any time, June."

That kiss, that little peck on the cheek. I bet you're a bit disappointed, that you think she should have fallen for me right then and there. But I wasn't, not one bit. She trusts me now, and that is never a small thing. Hell, I've got the rest of our lives to convince her that I'm the man for her. Now that's something to live for, something beyond survival, although I'm going to keep laughter on the list. You just gotta laugh.

And really, who is June? She's this wonderful, decidedly cute mystery to unwind. Pixie small and wicked with a gun, punching guys over twice her weight in the nose, and a sense of humor to boot. Now that's something to live for.

Let's just hope I'm smart enough... no, that's not right. Let's hope that *we're* smart enough to stay alive so our relationship can grow.

She grabs my hand and holds it until it's dark enough for us to embark on the next leg of our adventure... together.

EPISODE 2

WOODY AND JUNE VERSUS THE FUNGUS-HEAD ZOMBIES

More adventure, more zombies, and more Woody and June awaits you in.... *Woody and June versus the Fungus-Head Zombies*.

Coming soon on April 10, 2019

Join the Woody and June Fan Club at WoodyAndJune.com so you don't miss a thing (plus fun behind-the-scenes features and free stuff!).

WOODY AND JUNE VERSUS THE FUNGUS-HEAD ZOMBIES

Seriously? You Call This a First Date?

When Woody Beckman meets June Medina, neither expects the adventures that will follow. Dedicated go-it-alone survivors, they've learned not to trust anyone in post-zombie-apocalypse Arizona.

Woody thinks that June just might be too much for him. She's beautiful, smart, and way too good with a gun. Their jaunt to the Grand Canyon to put Woody's fungus theory of zombies to the test doesn't turn out quite like they expect and it will take everything they've got to survive.

They're learning to trust each other, but can they survive long enough to find out what's next for their relationship?

A story of adventure and love and taking things (even the apocalypse) in stride.

ABOUT THE AUTHOR

Robert J. McCarter is the author of six novels, three novellas, and dozens of short stories. He is a finalist for the *Writers of the Future* contest and his stories have appeared in *The Saturday Evening Post, Adomeda Spaceways Inflight Magazine, Everyday Fiction*, and numerous anthologies.

He has written a series of first person ghost novels (starting with Shuffled Off: A Ghost's Memoir) and a superhero / love story series (Neutrinoman and Lightningirl, A Love Story), as well as two short story collections.

Of his latest novel, *Seeing Forever*, Kirkus Reviews says, "Sci-fi as it should be: engaging, moving, and grand in scope."

Find out more at:
robertjmccarter.com

BOOKS BY ROBERT J. MCCARTER

WOODY AND JUNE VERSUS THE APOCALYPSE

1. Woody and June versus the Wannabe Warlord
2. Woody and June versus the Fungus-Head Zombies
   (*coming April, 2019*)
3. Woody and June versus the Grand Canyon
4. (*coming May, 2019*)
5. Woody and June versus the Ex
6. (*coming June, 2019*)
7. Woody and June versus the Third Wheel
8. (*coming July, 2019*)
9. Woody and June versus Phantom Company
10. (*coming August, 2019*)
11. Woody and June versus the Daring Rescue
12. (*coming September, 2019*)

Join the Woody and June Fan Club at WoodyAndJune.com

NOVELS IN THE "GHOST'S MEMOIR" WORLD:

- Shuffled Off: A Ghost's Memoir, Book 1
- Drawing the Dead
- To Be a Fool: A Ghost's Memoir, Book 2
- Of Things Not Seen: A Ghost's Memoir, Book 3

OTHER NOVELS:

- Seeing Forever

BOOKS IN THE NEUTRINOMAN AND LIGHTNINGIRL SERIES:

- Meteor Attack! Neutrinoman and Lightningirl, A Love Story. Episode 1
- Toxic Asset: Neutrinoman and Lightningirl, A Love Story. Episode 2
- Protocol X: Neutrinoman and Lightningirl, A Love Story. Episode 3
- Season 1 (Omnibus edition of Episodes 1 - 3)
- Off Book: Neutrinoman and Lightningirl, A Love Story. Episode 4 (*Coming soon*)

WALTER ANCHOR, GHOST DETECTIVE STORIES

- **Case 1: "Detecting Haley"** (part of *Life After: Stories of Life, Death, and the Places in Between*)
- **Case 2: "The Ghost Brides Gift"** (exclusive to newsletter subscribers)
- **Case 3: "A Long Hard Fall"** (coming in 2019)

*For a complete list of Walter Anchor stories, go to
RobertJMcCarter.com/WalterAnchor*

SHORT STORES AND COLLECTIONS

- Life After: Stories of Life, Death, and the Places in

Between

- Anomalous Readings: Thirteen Curious and Confounding Tales
- Probability: Resolve
- The Turing Test Will Be Televised
- Ghost Hacker, Zombie Maker

For a complete list, go to RobertJMcCarter.com

www.ingramcontent.com/pod-product-compliance
Lightning Source LLC
Chambersburg PA
CBHW020605130626
46552CB00007B/3052